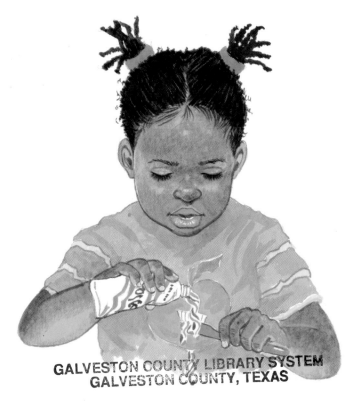

I don't eat
toothpaste
anymore!

HTS ✾ BOOKS™
AN IMPRINT OF FOREST HOUSE®
School & Library Edition

© Tamarind 1993   ISBN 1-870516-16-8   Printed in Singapore
This impression 1995   Library of Congress Number 93-27466

A catalogue reference for this book is available from the British Library

I used to be a baby.

But I'm big now.

don't throw my dinner on the floor ... OOPS!

I don't pull Mum's hair.

She pulls mine . . . OUCH!

Mum used to dress me.

Now I can dress myself.

I don't eat toothpaste anymore . . .

. . . and I can wash myself.

I used to go really slow.

Now I whizz along.

I tidy up . . .

. . . because I'm big now.

But not too big for a cuddle.